T
Magnific
Ride

Ma Vile
Vince Vile
Keith and Timothy Elastic
Barrington Small
Hodge the
Little Horror
Fabian Farquar
Seymour Potts
Elsie Potts
(and Gladys)

The Magnificent Misfits Ride Again

J.J. MURHALL

Illustrated by
Eleanor Taylor

This book is dedicated to
Michael and Saoirse Ruby,
and to all those 'misfits'
I have ever known,
including the most 'magnificent'
one of all – Alfie.
XX

First published in Great Britain in 1998
Bloomsbury Publishing Plc, 38 Soho Square, London, W1V 5DF

A CIP catalogue record of this book is available from the British Library

ISBN 0 7475 3645 7

Printed in England by Clays Ltd, St Ives plc

10 9 8 7 6 5 4 3 2 1

Cover design by Michelle Radford

One

Something very strange had happened to Miss Barnes, the class teacher. She'd rushed off to receive an urgent phone call, and had returned at least a foot taller. Her clothes were the same, but the class of 5b noticed that she'd now acquired a pair of extremely hairy legs and a strange look in one eye, and her hair, which she normally wore in a ponytail, was sticking out in all directions.

'Right, class,' said Miss Barnes, turning towards the blackboard. 'What does two and two make?'

5b could hardly believe their ears. Miss Barnes, was the strictest teacher at

St Gregorys, and she would never set such an easy question.

Miss Barnes swung around, her hair slipping oddly to one side. A few of the children giggled as she pushed it back. No one had ever realised that Miss Barnes wore a wig to school.

'Don't you know?' she snapped. 'Not very bright, are you?'

Suddenly Miss Barnes delved into her pocket and pulled out a packet of extra strong mints. She then proceeded to cram the whole lot into her mouth, crunching them noisily. The class watched, mesmerised, as her jaws moved up and down and round and round like a camel with a mouthful of bubble gum. Finally, she swallowed and taking a deep breath belted out:

'PICKLED ONIONS!' at the top of her voice, and banged her fist down hard on the table.

Sitting at the back of the class, Seymour

Potts and Barrington Small, the world's newest superheroes, and Magnificent Misfits for one whole week now, glanced knowingly at each other. The lady standing in front of them wasn't Miss Barnes at all. She, *he* was none other than Vince Vile, that master of disguise and all-round baddy from the planet Ghastly.

Seymour sighed. A superhero's work was never done. They'd only just got rid of Vince's grandma, Ma Vile, and now Vince had turned up looking for the power-packed pickled onions. What was it with people hell-bent on taking over the world – didn't they ever take a holiday?

'Hold on. I think I know the answer to this one,' whispered Barrington eagerly. He stuck his hand up in the air. Vince Vile stared at him disdainfully.

'Do two and two pickled onions make four?' asked Barrington, looking very pleased with himself. This was the first time he'd ever known the answer to one of

Miss Barnes' questions and having done some minor calculations on his fingers, he was sure he must be right.

Seymour kicked him under the table.

'Ssh. We don't want to draw attention to ourselves,' he muttered, and beneath his desk he fumbled with the catch on his "Miskit" box and pulled out his mobile

phone. He needed to contact the other Magnificent Misfits. His sister Elsie and the Elastic twins were in the class below, and Seymour had a good idea where Fabian might be. He quickly dialled his number. If Fabian Farquar wasn't in school, you were sure to find him in the 'SoapSuds' launderette. Fabian's hobby was doing his washing, and the launderette was his second home. The woman who ran it always saved him a dryer and gave him a cup of tea whenever he turned up.

'Fabian Farquar, Magnificent Misfit, speaking,' said Fabian, answering his mobile snootily as he watched his dryer go around.

'It's me. Seymour,' whispered Seymour, ducking down behind his desk. 'We've got trouble here. Vince Vile has disguised himself as Miss Barnes and he's going on about the pickled onions. I've put them in my locker but I don't know how safe they'll be in there. I never in a million years thought Vince Vile would turn up at St Gregorys looking for them.' He glanced up. Vince was now moving from child to child, asking them whether they knew the whereabouts of a certain jar.

'You'd better get back here,' hissed Seymour.

'But I can't,' said Fabian huffily. 'I haven't finished drying my Misfit suit yet.'

'Well hurry up then,' urged Seymour. He was just about to call the others when he felt the presence of a tall figure looming over him. Slowly, Seymour looked up. Vince Vile was staring down at him, his glass eye gleaming coldly like a marble.

'Having a nice chat?' he asked dryly.

'I was just ringing my mum, er, miss,' gulped Seymour, giving him a friendly smile, 'to tell her I'll be late home tonight.'

Vince Vile shook his head. 'I don't know what the world's coming to. Kids with mobile phones. It'll be kids with cars next.

You lot have never had it so good.' His eyes narrowed. 'But of course all that will change. What children really need is discipline and hard work. Someone who'll rule you all and turn you into Kidults.' Vince Vile leant closer to Seymour. 'Know anything about a jar of pickled onions, sonny?'

Seymour shook his head and said nothing. He knew *exactly* what a Kidult was. If the pickles fell into the wrong hands and were taken to the planet Ghastly, this harmless-looking jar could turn all the worlds' children into their parents overnight. The girls would become their dads and the boys, their mums. They'd be made to work day and night, and Christmas and birthdays would be banned. Parents would disappear and turn up on the planet Swampsack, which was the gloomiest, dreariest place in the whole universe. There they would live, constantly mowing the grass that grew like

crazy and avoiding the crocodiles that roamed freely around. Swampsack was also shrinking, so eventually everyone's mum and dad would fall off it and drift away into space, never to be seen again.

Seymour thought of the powerful jar in his locker, tucked in between his maths book and a packet of stale crisps. He hoped it was safe.

Suddenly, a small boy called Reggie Brown put his hand up. 'Excuse me, Miss Barnes, but there's a twenty pound note stuck to the bottom of your shoe.' Vince Vile prised the note off his high heel and slapped it into Reggie's hand. 'Here, kid. Get yourself a decent haircut,' he declared, staring at Reggie's appalling hairstyle, that was spiky on top, feathery at the bottom and was bleached blond.

'After all, there's plenty more where that came from,' and Vince slammed a large holdall, that was bulging at the seams, down on his desk. The class gasped as he unzipped it. Inside it was stuffed full of money.

'Miss Barnes has been a very naughty teacher,' announced Vince Vile, straining to shut the bag. 'She's robbed a bank and shortly the police will arrive to arrest her.' He bundled the holdall beneath his arm and surveyed the class. 'Actually, it was *me* who did it. Your real teacher's locked in the store cupboard,' he grinned, showing off his enormous yellow teeth. 'Now I've got some cash, I just need the onions. *Then* the world will be *mine*. My trusty helpers, Lumpy and Gretch, overheard someone talking in the pub. It's rumoured that The Magnificent Misfits who guard the jar might be schoolkids in disguise, though I doubt it. Kids could never be superheroes. They're just too darn short.' And with that he raced out of the door.

5b erupted. It was supposed to be maths that morning, nothing as exciting as this, and everyone started to scream and shout and muck about. All except Reggie Brown who studied his new-found fortune intently to see if it was fake.

While all the excitement was going on, Seymour and Barrington took the opportunity to change. They slipped behind a screen that the real Miss Barnes had erected for the "Tudor" project 5b was working on, and pulled out the Space Hoppers from their Miskit boxes.

'We've got to stop Vince. If he gets his greedy mitts on the pickles, all us kids are doomed,' panted Seymour, as he breathlessly inflated his machine. 'We can wave goodbye to having fun and say hello to horrible hard work.'

Barrington nodded in agreement, and pulling his beloved teddy bear Simon from his blazer pocket, he put him inside his Miskit box and then quickly clambered out of his school uniform.

The Magnificent Misfits always wore their 'Misfit' outfits under their clothes. It saved time, not to mention embarrassment. After all, what self-respecting ten year old wants to show their knickers off in public?

Next, Seymour rang his sister and the Elastic twins. They were in the middle of a PE lesson and halfway up a jungle gym when the call came. Mr Spittle, the PE teacher, was not very pleased when all three of them suddenly developed the most terrible stomach ache, but after some convincing, they managed to get away and change in the toilets. Gladys, Elsie's imaginary friend went to. Elsie would never go anywhere without her, especially on a superhero saving mission and possibly into space.

Meanwhile, back in 5b, Seymour opened a window, then he and Barrington stepped out from behind the screen. The whole class turned and gazed in amazement as the two Magnificent Misfits made their way across the classroom with their Space Hoppers and Miskits tucked under each arm.

'We've just flown in,' announced Seymour, indicating towards the open window behind the screen. 'I understand there's been a bit of bother.'

'That's right,' replied Reggie Brown, twiddling his little gold earring excitedly.

'Some bloke's disguised himself as our teacher and pinned a bank job on her. Now

he's run off with a bag full of money. Great, innit?'

When they reached the door, Seymour and Barrington turned to face 5b, with their hands firmly on their hips. The class stared at them in adoration as the two gazed out from beneath their hoods.

'Never fear. The Misfits are here,' declared Seymour proudly, as he and Barrington stepped out into the corridor.

Looking both ways, they could see that it was empty. Seymour put a finger to his lips as 5b clamoured to try and peer over his shoulder. He'd sprinkled some Power Powder over his cereal for breakfast, and his sense of hearing was once again as sharp as a razor. Seymour listened intently as the voice of Miss Barnes called out faintly,

'Help! Help! Let me out at once!'

Barrington stared at Seymour and then pointed further down the corridor to where the lockers stood. Cautiously, the Magnificent Misfits made their way towards them with the whole class following close behind. Every locker door, including Seymour's, was now hanging off its hinges and all of Seymour's belongings, along with his precious collection of sweet wrappers, were scattered over the floor. Seymour and Barrington peered inside the locker, fearing the worst. Sure enough, it was empty and the jar was gone, and on the floor lay an empty packet of extra-strong mints. Up ahead, the doors to the playground swung backwards and forwards, creaking loudly.

'Right, 5b. The jar is missing,' said Seymour, bending down and picking up the mint wrapper. This would certainly be one for his collection.

Once again Reggie Brown put up his hand. 'Er, excuse me, Mr Magnificent, but that locker you looked in belongs to a right weirdo called Seymour Potts. In fact, he and his fat mate have both disappeared. Do you think they're involved? Or maybe they just got scared and ran away.' And he sniggered to himself.

Seymour glanced nervously at Barrington, who pulled his hood further down over his eyes and held in his stomach in case he was recognised.

'I've no idea. I'm a superhero, not Sherlock Holmes,' replied Seymour brusquely. 'But we've had trouble with

Vince's grandma already this week, so we can't stand around chatting all day. There's a whole wide world to save out there, and we're the ones to do it.' With that, both he and Barrington turned quickly on their heels and hurried towards the playground.

Reggie glanced at the store cupboard. 'Shall we let Barmy Barnes out now?' he suggested, staring at the rest of the class, who didn't look too eager.

Reggie shrugged.

'OK, maybe later then,' he smiled, and they all raced back to their classroom to see whether that strange man had left any more money lying around.

Through the gym window Mr Spittle watched like a lovesick puppy as Vince Vile hitched up his dress, hurried out of the school gates and into a waiting ice-cream van. He thought the divine Miss Barnes was looking particularly beautiful this morning and he sighed, hoping that she didn't actually fancy an ice-cream seller. It would break his heart. He also wondered what that bunch of superheroes were doing charging across the playground as well. But he didn't stop to find out. Seymour Potts, Barrington Small and that laundry fanatic Fabian Farquar were in Miss Barnes' class. Mr Spittle loathed them all, and if 5b had been left unattended, this could be the perfect opportunity to catch them up to no good and finally get them expelled.

Two

People in the street stopped what they were doing and watched The Magnificent Misfits fly high overhead. They were pursuing a battered old ice-cream van that was diving and swooping above the rooftops. It had four bald tyres, huge glass wings and a sign that read: STOP! MIND THAT ALIEN! plastered across the back.

The Misfits were becoming very well known by now, even though everyone tried to avoid them, mainly because they'd insist on saving people when they didn't need to be saved, and also because they'd dropped someone once in mid-flight and he'd had a very narrow escape. One teenage boy in particular had been happily

walking down the street, when he was scooped up by Seymour, flown back home and made to change his shoes.

His crime? The Magnificent Misfits were very concerned that he might trip over his undone trainer laces and hurt himself.

'But that's how I like 'em, man,' the boy had insisted as they'd marched him upstairs to his bedroom.

'Sorry. But they're far too dangerous,'

scolded Fabian. 'Here. Try these.' And he picked out a sensible pair of wellingtons from the back of the boy's wardrobe and thrust them at him. The boy hadn't worn those horrible things since he was a kid, but he'd squeezed his feet into them anyway, just to get rid of these nagging superheroes. That tall, skinny one with the jet-black hair was especially rude. He kept wrinkling his nose up at the piles of crumpled clothes all over the carpet and tutting loudly.

'Just remember, we'll be watching out for you,' Seymour had called, waving at him and smiling from across the road as the teenager had eventually hobbled off shamefaced to meet his friends.

Fabian Farquar had also been watching his fellow Misfits from the steamy windows of the 'SoapSuds' launderette. He was rather annoyed that they'd left without him, but he guessed that Vince Vile must have got his hands on the onions because his ice-cream van was travelling at some speed. Fabian knew he'd have to hurry – it wouldn't be long before Vince and the Misfits left the earth's atmosphere and were halfway to the planet Ghastly.

Fabian turned around and tapped a spotty-looking boy wearing a drab green anorak sharply on the hand. Ninian Soames, superhero expert and all-round nosy parker quickly tossed Fabian's starched white underpants back in the laundry basket and grinned sheepishly.

Ninian had in fact been looking for clues, because he was not convinced that the Magnificent Misfits were real superheroes at all. Everywhere Fabian turned lately, Ninian was never far behind. Fabian gave him one of his famous Farquar glares to get rid of him and Ninian fled from the launderette, clutching his Superhero scrapbook to his chest.

Fabian's Misfit costume was now clean and dry but he needed to change without being seen. So, glancing over his shoulder to make sure no one was looking, he picked up his Miskit box and climbed into one of the dryers. Inside it was a bit cramped and he kept on swinging from side to side, but eventually Fabian managed to wriggle into his outfit. Inflating his Space Hopper proved a problem though, as once it was blown up it was almost as big as the dryer itself. But finally he managed to shove it through the door and then scramble out afterwards.

Smoothing down the front of his suit, Fabian walked calmly across the floor.

People couldn't believe their eyes. Had they really just seen a superhero climbing out of a tumble dryer? A few of them hurried over to the machine and peered cautiously inside just in case another one might pop out.

Outside on the pavement, Fabian climbed aboard his Space Hopper and took off after his friends, and with his tight white suit gleaming in the sunshine, he looked exactly like a washing powder advert streaking across the clear blue sky.

Three

Space was dark. *Very* dark indeed, and the Magnificent Misfits were all afraid of the dark. Back home, Barrington always slept with the landing light on, and with his teddy bear Simon. So he was glad he'd brought him along today, because even though there was the occasional star to light the way, the deeper the Misfits travelled into space, the blacker it became.

'Omonoslomo could have put some headlights on these machines,' moaned Keith, referring to their mighty ruler who lived on the planet Twart, which was situated to the right of them and many thousand light years away.

'I can't see where I'm going,' complained

Timothy Elastic, who whinged slightly less than his brother, but not much. 'There could be a planet up ahead and I wouldn't even know.'

'You'd notice that one. Look!' cried Elsie. Elsie Potts had been given the power to shout louder than anyone else in the whole universe, and a passing meteorite vibrated with the shock of her voice.

She pointed up ahead. In the distance the brightly-coloured planet of Ghastly could be seen, then it disappeared, then appeared again.

As the Misfits neared Ghastly and prepared to land, they could see that it was just as Omonoslomo had described: one huge neon sign.

Every building, every lamp-post and even the pavements, were lit up like a twenty-four hour disco. There were no trees, only plastic ones and they were illuminated as well. Strung across the streets were rows of fairy lights. In fact, there wasn't a single centimetre of Ghastly that wasn't flashing on and off at an alarming rate.

The place was teaming with aliens. They looked like humans, except they were taller, thinner, and their skin was slightly orange. Everyone was talking at the same time, and they were dressed in loud coloured shirts with palm trees on them, tiger-print trouser suits or something equally bright.

The Magnificent Misfits landed in a spaceship car park, where all the vehicles seemed to be either pink or purple and had stickers with I'VE BEEN TO MARS or I LUV STARS stuck on their bumpers and windscreens. There was no sign of the Vile Van, they'd lost sight of it just after passing Pluto. It may have looked clapped out, but, boy could it shift.

Seymour, the Elastic twins, Elsie and Barrington all stared through the flashing lights and up into the sky hoping to see Fabian heading towards them. But the sky was empty except for a few spaceships hovering overhead, and the occasional shooting star whizzing by.

'Where's Fabian?' Seymour sighed. 'We need all the help we can get right now.'

'He's probably still doing his washing,' tutted Keith, frowning.

'Yeah. Typical Fabian,' added Keith's

brother, plonking himself down on his Space Hopper. 'His head stuck in a tumble dryer and never around when you need him.'

Suddenly, a man dressed in a silver suit and carrying a clipboard, ran towards them.

'Passport control,' he declared. 'Identify yourselves.'

The Magnificent Misfits rummaged

inside their Miskit boxes and pulled out their special Misfit passports. After studying them, and having a bit of a giggle at the Elastic twin's photographs, the man handed them back.

'So you're superheroes, then,' he said peering at them over the top of his mirrored sunglasses. 'We get a lot of them up here. They're usually looking for one of the Vile family. Ma Vile, Vince, or his nephew, Hodge, the biggest brat this side of Venus.'

The Misfits looked at each other anxiously.

'You mean there's *another* member of the Vile family on the loose?' said Barrington, glancing nervously over his shoulder.

The man nodded and pointed up at the sky. 'You see that monstrosity over there?' He indicated towards an oblong shape. 'Well, *that's* Hodge's toy box. It's so big that it's now been classified as a planet all of its own. Hodge the little Horror, he's called, and if you ever meet him you'll know why.'

'Actually, it's Vince Vile we're looking for,' said Seymour who was pleasantly surprised that at least some of the inhabitants of Ghastly seemed friendly. He'd always imagined other planets to be uninviting places with scary-looking aliens who'd tie you up and stick pins in your toes.

'Vince Vile lives up on the huge plastic mound just outside town, in a house called *Notdunroamin*,' replied the passport controller. 'You can't miss it, just follow the multi-coloured street signs. What's he been up to this time? Trying to take over the world again, is he? It was the moon last month, only when he landed he was extremely cross because it's uninhabited. Any fool could have told him that. He came back carrying a tatty-looking flag with Stars and Stripes on it, and he's stuck it in his front garden. He and his grandma

are really giving our planet a bad name. We're trying to get a tourist trade up here, you see, but no one wants to visit because of them. Anyway, I must be off. There's a star bus landing in a few minutes. Good Ghastly day to you.' And he hurried away, leaving Seymour and the others to head off in the opposite direction.

When they reached the brow of the

enormous hill, the Misfits could see that it was covered in bright green plastic grass and that Vince's house stood alone, perched high on top. It was painted gold, and at each window hung sickly pink frilly curtains the colour of candyfloss. All around the front was a border of plastic flowers and stuck in the middle of the lawn was the American flag that Vince had stolen from the moon.

'Oh, isn't it sweet,' declared Barrington. 'Not at all how you'd imagine it to be.'

The Magnificent Misfits tiptoed slowly towards one of the windows and peeped inside. Vince was sprawled on a large purple sofa, drinking a cocktail through a straw. By his side were a box of mints, and every now and then he'd toss a couple into his mouth.

'Shall we wait until Vince is asleep and then break in?' asked Barrington.

Seymour shook his head. 'We'll confront him face to face. Remember, Barrington, the Magnificent Misfits are brave and fearless.'

'Are we?' replied Barrington, looking rather bemused as he and the others followed Seymour towards the front door.

Seymour rang the bell. It played the Ghastly National Anthem twice over before the door was opened by Lumpy and Gretch. Both of them were short, dumpy, bald-headed and dressed in stripy pyjamas. They were almost identical, except that Gretch's face looked as if it had been flattened by a frying pan more times than Lumpy's.

'Da Boss is expectin' yer,' said Lumpy, leading the Misfits into the living room, where the zebra-striped wallpaper did nothing to enhance the leopard-print carpet.

'Well, well, well. We meet at last, Magnificent Misfits,' declared Vince, regarding them coldly from the depths of his sofa. He'd changed into his hideous jacket and frilly shirt now, and looked more like the photograph that Omonoslomo had first shown them back on the planet Twart.

'But one of you is missing. What happened? Did he fall off his big balloon on the way here?' Vince threw back his head and laughed loudly, showing off a mouthful of mashed-up mints.

'Where's the pickles, Mr Vile?' asked Seymour, stepping forward bravely.

'The jar is quite safe. It's not time to use them yet,' replied Vince, sucking the dregs of his cocktail noisily. 'The power of the pickles will only work when Ghastly is directly opposite earth.' Vince glanced at his chunky gold watch. 'Which should be in about an hour.'

Seymour and the others stared out of the window towards the planet that was their home. At the moment it was situated a little to the right of Ghastly. It looked tiny and very much alone.

'Why can't you keep your hands off the world? What's it ever done to you?' Asked Elsie, putting her arm protectively around Gladys.

Vince stared at her, sucking thoughtfully on another extra-strong mint. 'Because when I was a little boy I had a globe of the world,' he replied miserably. 'I loved that globe more than anything. But one day my wicked old grandmama took it away, aimed it towards Swampsack and kicked it into orbit. She wouldn't let me have any toys, you see, and all I had to play with was a set of her old false teeth.'

'I know how you feel,' replied Barrington despondently. 'I wanted a 'Playstation' for Christmas, but my gran wouldn't let me.'

'That doesn't excuse your behaviour, Mr Vile,' replied Seymour sternly.

Vince shrugged. 'Listen, Misfit. I'm bad. I've *always* been bad. And a bad boy I will stay. In precisely forty-five minutes I shall become the Top Dog. The Big Cheese. The Bees Knees. The KING OF THE WORLD!! And there's not a thing you can do about it.'

He waved a hand towards Lumpy and Gretch. 'Tie these mongrels up, boys. I'm so bored with interfering superheroes.'

As quick as a flash the little sidekicks pressed a button on the wall and the ceiling slid open. The Misfits had no time to move, as in an instant, a large net dropped directly on to them. It looked as fine as cotton, but was as strong as steel, and the more the Misfits tried to free themselves the more ensnared they became.

'Just one of my little traps,' chuckled Vince, heading towards the door.

'Let's just hope your missing Misfit mate

doesn't decide to have a sniff of my flowers if he turns up. They give off my hideous Vile Vapour and he'll be sleeping like a baby for a thousand years if he does. Toodle-loo.' And he went off with Lumpy and Gretch, leaving the Magnificent Misfits well and truly trapped.

'I've no idea where Fabian is,' remarked Seymour, becoming more tangled up every time he tried to move. 'I've tried him on his mobile, but it must be switched off.

I wish he'd hurry up. Anyway, at least we know that he definitely won't sniff those flowers. With his hayfever, even walking past a florist brings tears to his eyes.' Seymour glanced at Barrington who had begun to wriggle and jiggle about like a trapped sardine.

'You must have taken your Power Powder this morning, Barrington. Why don't you use your super strength to get us out of this mess?'

Barrington bit his bottom lip and then,

crossing his knees, he looked imploringly at Seymour. 'That's the problem. I don't think I can do anything at the moment. You see, I drank *four* glasses of coke when I took my Power Powder, and now I *really* need to go to the toilet!'

Seymour rolled his eyes in exasperation. 'Well for goodness sake hold on Barrington. Because superheroes most definitely do not, I repeat, do not WET THEMSELVES, OK?'

Barrington nodded, and closing his eyes tightly he gritted his teeth as if his very life depended on it.

Four

Fabian had landed! And hiding behind a parked spaceship, he'd seen everything. His amazing eyesight power was working to full effect and he could see Vince Vile and his trusty helpers heading down the hill towards him. Fabian ducked further down as the sound of Vince's voice got nearer.

They were off to tell Ma Vile that it was time to hang up her pension book and retire as the universe's oldest villain. Vince was even threatening to stick her in an old alien's home.

'I've finally beaten the old bat once and for all,' Vince chuckled to Lumpy and Gretch as they passed close by and rounded the corner.

Fabian stood up. He was still a bit cross that the others had left him behind, but he knew he couldn't let them down, and flicking the teeniest speck of moon dust from his sleeve he set off to rescue them.

No one was more pleased to see Fabian climbing in through an open window than Barrington, whose face was now turning various shades of pink as he bounced up and down on his heels in desperation.

'What kept you? Seymour tried to call you!' moaned Keith, who was squashed against his frowning brother.

'Well *excuse me*!' scoffed Fabian, rubbing the end of his nose lightly. 'But I did have rather a long way to travel you know. *And* I had to guess which direction you'd gone in. Besides,' he said, looking a little sheepish, 'I've left my mobile in the tumble drier.' He sniffed the air lightly as he set about untangling his friends.

'Those pongy-looking flowers outside look like they're made of plastic, but I'm sure they'd have made me sneeze like mad if I'd had the slightest sniff of them.'

'They'd have done more than that, Fabian,' replied Seymour, ducking beneath the net like a contortionist as his friend began to ease it over his head. 'Those flowers contain a sleeping gas called Vile Vapour. You'd have ended up having the longest lie-in in history if you'd had so much as a whiff. Anyway, it's a good job you turned up when you did, 'cause we must find the pickled onion jar before Vince gets back – we've got about twenty minutes before the power of the pickles starts to take effect!'

After some careful pulling and a few tangled feet and fingers, Fabian finally managed to unravel the other Misfits, and the net was bundled up and shoved in the corner like an enormous ball of knitting.

'I'll go and look in the toilet,' said Barrington, hastily trotting off as everyone set about searching for the pickled onion jar.

Seymour glanced up at the clock on the wall. It read ten to twelve. Outside, the earth had almost drawn level with Ghastly. 'Quick – Vince will be back any moment,' he said, throwing cushions on to the floor as he stuck his hand down the back of the sofa, just in case Vince had somehow managed to hide it down there. However, the only things that he pulled out were some Ghastly coins, a dog-eared magazine about flying saucers, and half a packet of extra-strong mints.

The minutes ticked by, but the jar was nowhere to be found. Suddenly Fabian spotted an enormous cupboard on top of some shelves. It was very high up and out

of reach. 'Maybe it's in there,' he suggested.

Seymour nodded, and turned to Barrington, who had come back from the toilet looking very relieved. 'Barrington. You've been given the power to be as agile as a cat. Climb up and take a look,' he said urgently.

Barrington sighed. This climbing about lark was becoming a bit too much like hard work. He wished Omonoslomo had given him the power to sit around all day doing nothing instead. He'd have been *really* good at that. However, he put one foot gingerly on the cocktail cabinet, and the other on the bottom shelf and began to climb.

The Elastic twins jumped up and down with their big, baggy hoods falling over their eyes as they watched him eagerly make his ascent. Suddenly they began to sniff the air.

'We can smell mints. Extra-strong ones,'

they declared, their noses working faster than a sniffer dog's on the scent of his dinner. Elsie rushed over to the window. 'It's Vince! He's coming up the path!' she cried, her voice shattering a nearby glass.

The Magnificent Misfits stared nervously at each other.

'I want to go home!' exclaimed Timothy.

'So do I!' wailed his brother. And everyone looked towards the front door as the sound of Vince's key turned in the lock.

Barrington had almost reached the top shelf when Vince walked into the room. He was moaning to Lumpy and Gretch about the black eye that his gran had just given him, when he stopped in his tracks.

'DON'T TOUCH THAT CUPBOARD!!' he roared, charging towards Barrington, just as he opened it, lost his footing and swung like a monkey from the cupboard door. Instantly, an avalanche of mints came pouring out, and rained down on Vince

like hailstones, until after a few endless minutes he was buried up to his neck in a mountain of them. Suddenly, the cupboard door gave way, and Barrington fell, pulling the shelf and everything on it with him.

Bottles and ornaments went crashing around his ears, as Barrington landed on the sofa, bounced off, tripped over the rug and then stumbled towards the window. Grabbing hold of the curtains, he gave them a tug. There was a loud rip and then a creaking sound as the window frame fell forward, pulling half the wall away with it. Barrington coughed and spluttered as brick dust and rubble engulfed him. He blundered around, knocked over a lamp stand, skidded on something slippery, fell on to a drinks trolley, spun across the floor, knocked Lumpy and Gretch off their feet like skittles, smashed into the opposite wall, knocked down another shelf-load of tacky ornaments, slid back, ran over Seymour's foot, grabbed hold of the armchair, leapt on to it, did a somersault, and landed on the other side of the room, breathless and bewildered.

'Blimey. That Power Powder's strong stuff,' he declared, leaning against a wall to catch his breath. Everyone stared in amazement as it began to tilt slowly backwards, finally crashing to the ground as the ceiling caved in and Barrington stumbled out into the garden .

When the dust had settled, the only thing that didn't appear smashed, squashed, bent or battered was the furthest wall. It remained standing surrounded now by a backdrop of sky and stars.

'I told you to give up those mints, Your Vileness,' declared Gretch, shaking his head woefully.

'I was *trying*. I'm down to twenty packets a day now, ' wailed Vince.

'But I thought I'd put a few tons by for emergencies, and *now* look what's happened. My state of the art living room's been demolished and I've been buried alive by my secret sweetie stash.' And he began shovelling through them.

'Not so fast, Mr Vile,' said Elsie, picking up a big dented bucket, and tipping the contents over his head.

'You little fool,' spluttered Vince, as a thick grey mixture began to ooze slowly over him. 'That's quick-drying cement. Lumpy and Gretch were going to crazy-pave my patio with it. Now they'll have to rebuild my living room instead.'

'Well. It serves you right,' scoffed Elsie. 'You and your grandma should stop all this world domination nonsense and give each other a nice big kiss instead.'

Vince sneered at her, shuddering at the thought.

Suddenly, Seymour spotted something lying amongst the debris. Walking over to the upturned drinks trolley, he saw that nestled beneath it was the precious jar of pickled onions. Seymour scooped it up.

The lid had come loose, but amazingly it was still intact.

'You were supposed to put the pickles in the safe,' moaned Vince, glowering at Lumpy and Gretch.

Lumpy shrugged. 'Sorry, Oh Vile One, but we forgot der code. Gretch kept finkin' it was three two one. An' I fort it woz one one one. So we put der pickles in der plant pot instead.'

'It was one two three!! You useless twerps!!' roared Vince in exasperation as

Seymour carefully placed the jar in his Miskit box.

Lumpy and Gretch put their hands up as the Elastic twins whipped out their Slapper Blappers and stood guard over them both.

'Don't shoot!' they gulped, backing away. 'We don't like guns.'

'Me neither. They're nasty, noisy things,' replied Keith. He took a deep breath, preparing for a moan. 'In fact. I really hate

these ones in particular. They're far too heavy. They make a funny squelching noise when you fire them, and they're messy as well. People think that being a superhero is really flash, but it isn't, unless you're Batman of course. *He's* got much better equipment than we have, *and* he drives a really ace car. Me and my brother are thinking of giving up this superhero stuff. We never get our homework done on time 'cause we're out saving someone or other, *and* we've missed two episodes of 'Star Trek' already this week.'

Lumpy and Gretch wished he'd shut up. Not even Vince moaned this much. Timothy was just about to join in as well when Seymour ordered everyone to gather up their Space Hoppers and prepare for take off.

As the Misfits rose high up into the night sky, Lumpy and Gretch hurried over to Vince. He looked like a statue. The cement was now rock hard and starting to crack.

'Just you wait. I'll hunt those mangy Misfits down,' seethed Vince, as Lumpy and Gretch began to chip away at his face. 'And then I'll *never*, EVER eat another mint again!!'

Five

The Magnificent Misfits landed behind the bike sheds of St Gregorys and quickly put their school clothes back on. Breathlessly, they all ran across the empty playground, with their ties undone and shirt-tails flying. Seymour checked his watch. It read ten-fifteen. Amazingly, they'd only been gone for twenty minutes, and hadn't even missed morning break.

As they crashed through the double doors that led to the corridor, Seymour could still hear Miss Barnes calling out from the store cupboard. Barrington unlocked it and his teacher stumbled out. She looked extremely cross and scowled at Barrington. Miss Barnes didn't have time

to explain what had happened to her, though, because a moment later Mr Spittle came marching up the corridor flanked by two police officers. He'd been about to let her out earlier, only a child had rushed in and told him that the police were in the playground searching for a criminal. Imagine Mr Spittle's surprise when the description had fitted that of Miss Barnes! And he could hardly believe his ears when they arrested her on suspicion of being a bank robber. He was beginning to have his doubts about asking her out on a date now.

A hardened criminal for a girlfriend? Mr Spittle shuddered at the thought. Whatever would his mother say?

Everyone watched as Miss Barnes was carted off to the police station. Seymour thought he would explain everything to the police later when he was back in his Misfit disguise. But until then he decided to let his teacher stew for a while. Miss Barnes was never very nice to him, and she was especially horrible to Barrington, always making him look a fool in front of the whole class. She and Mr Spittle deserved each other.

Seymour glanced up at the PE teacher who glared back down at him.

'And *where* have you lot been?' he scowled, looking at each of them in turn.

'You wouldn't believe us if we told you, sir,' replied Seymour politely.

Mr Spittle eyed them suspiciously. 'Elsie Potts and you Elastic boys seem to have made a miraculous recovery! Now run along to your classrooms, all of you, and just remember, I'll be watching you!'

Seymour and his friends headed off up the corridor. They had almost reached the lockers when Mr Spittle shouted for them to stop. Pointing towards Seymour's feet, he snapped, 'What on earth have you got on under your trousers, boy?'

Seymour peered down to see that the bottoms of his lime green Misfit tights were clearly visible.

'They're thermals, sir. Thermal underpants,' replied Seymour hastily.

Mr Spittle frowned. 'Thermals? In *June*?'

Seymour shrugged. 'Well, you never know when you might need a sudden change of clothing, sir.' He winked at his friends and gave Mr Spittle one of his special smiles.

'After all, life is full of surprises.'